ABCs
at the Beach

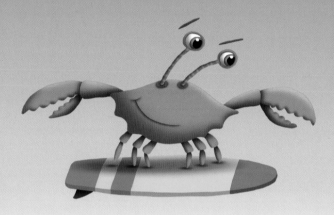

by Jennifer Marino Walters

illustrated by Nathan Y. Jarvis

RED CHAIR
•PRESS•

Egremont, Massachusetts

It looks like a good day to go the beach!

How many things can we find from A to Z?

Will we see **A**lligators or **B**unnies?

Maybe crafty **C**rows or dancing **D**inosaurs?

Look! It's an **anchor**—**Ahoy**!

Make way for the **beach ball**—bounce, bounce!

Be careful **crab.** Here comes Officer Max
in his **Dune buggy**—vroom, vroom!

Exercise is fun on the beach!

Flip-flops worn on sandy **feet**.

Go away, **gulls**!

Hey! That's my **hat**!

Let's go for **Ice cream**—yum!

Dive down in the water and you might see **jiggly jellyfish** and wavy **kelp**.

Never fear, if you need help! A **lifeguard** will save you! Lifeguards keep their **muscles** strong to swim far and fast!

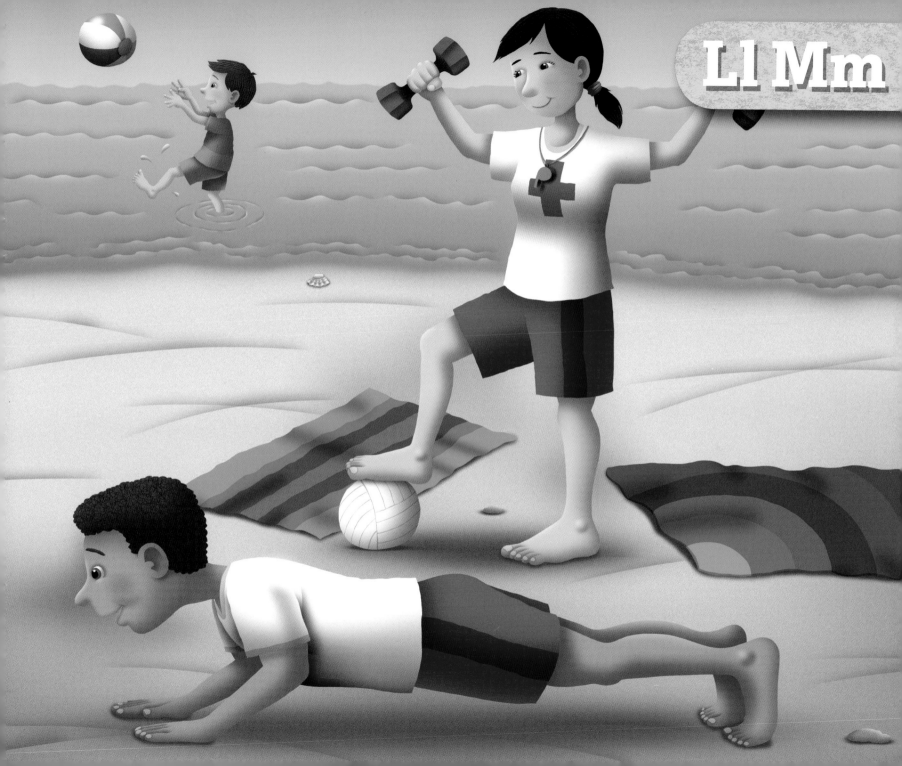

But if you are like me, I prefer to take a **nap** on the beach! If one thing is for sure, the **ocean** will still be there when I awaken.

Pink, blue or yellow, use your **pail** to build a castle. Now here's one **queen** who doesn't need a crown! This Queen conch is a big sea snail.

Rocks and **seashells** all around!

Now we can finish our **sandcastle**.

Towels and **umbrellas** keep us cool on the hot sand.

Hey, let's play **volleyball**!

Wild waves crash on shore.

Does **X** mark the spot for buried treasure?

This was a fun day at the beach. Now the **yellow** sun is setting low. It's time to say good-bye to the colorful **Zebrafish**. But we will be back soon.

The beach is full of fun from A to Z.

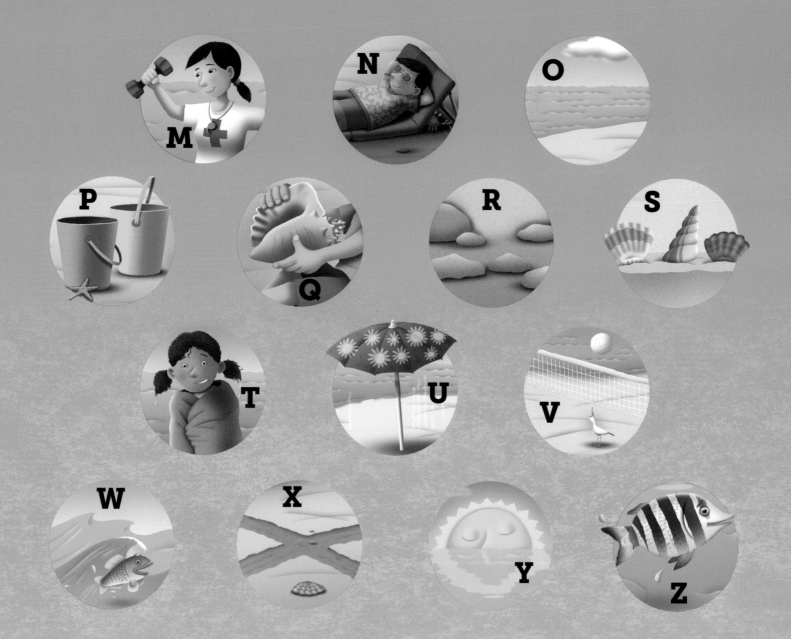

Publisher's Cataloging-In-Publication Data

Names: Marino Walters, Jennifer, author. | Jarvis, Nathan Y., illustrator.
Title: ABCs at the beach / by Jennifer Marino Walters ; illustrated by
Nathan Y. Jarvis.

Description: Egremont, Massachusetts : Red Chair Press, [2020] | Series:
[ABC adventures] | Interest age level: 004-008. | Includes a glossary-
style review of all the letters and items found in the book. | Summary:
"A fun and colorful day at the beach. Check the lively illustrations
for things that start with each letter of the alphabet. How many can
you see?"--Provided by publisher.

Identifiers: ISBN 9781634408813 (hardcover) | ISBN 9781634408820 (ebook)

Subjects: LCSH: Beaches--Juvenile fiction. | English language--Alphabet--
Juvenile fiction. | CYAC: Beaches--Fiction. | English language--
Alphabet--Fiction. | LCGFT: Alphabet books.

Classification: LCC PZ7.1.W358 Abb 2020 (print) | LCC PZ7.1.W358 (ebook) |
DDC [E]--dc23

LCCN: 2019937773

Printed in the United States of America

919-1P-CGS20